Kai's Journey to Gold Mountain

An Angel Island Story

By Katrina Saltonstall Currier

Illustrated by Gabhor Utomo

The poem on page 27 is borrowed from Lai, Lim, and Yung's *Island: Poetry and History of Chinese Immigrants on Angel Island, 1910-1940,* 1980, University of Washington Press. Reprinted by permission of the University of Washington Press.

Angel Island Association
P.O. Box 866
Tiburon CA 94920
www.angelisland.org 415.435.3522

ISBN 0-9667352-4-2 (soft cover)
ISBN 0-9667352-7-7 (hard cover)

Library of Congress Cataloging-in-Publication Data

Currier, Katrina Saltonstall, 1969-
Kai's journey to Gold Mountain: an Angel Island Story / by Katrina Saltonstall Currier.
p. cm.
Summary: In 1934, twelve-year-old Kai leaves China to join his father in America, but first he must take a long sea voyage, then endure weeks of crowded conditions and harsh examinations on Angel Island, fearing that he or his new friend will be sent home.
ISBN 0-9667352-4-2 (alk. paper) (soft cover)
ISBN 0-9667352-7-7 (hard cover)
1. Chinese Americans—Juvenile fiction. [1. Chinese Americans —Fiction. 2. Emigration and immigration—Fiction. 3. Immigrants—Fiction.
4. Angel Island (Calif.)—History—20th century—Fiction. 5. Los Angeles
(Calif.)—History—20th century—Fiction.] I. Title.
PZ7.C9356Kai 2005
[Fic]—dc22

2004014821

To Albert "Kai" Wong –
Thank you for sharing your story.

“Goodbye, China”

“Goodbye, China,” Kai whispered. His belly twisted into a knot. The engines of the *S.S. Hoover* rumbled, pulling the giant steamship slowly out of the harbor. Kai reached into his pocket and fingered the worn edges of the last letter from his father. “*Gum San*.” Kai repeated the two words he had thought about so often since receiving this letter. The knot in his belly twisted even tighter, but he forced a smile towards his new home. “Here I come, Gold Mountain. Here I come, America.”

Kai stood at the rail of the huge, black ship with the wind billowing through his loose trousers. Buttoning his tunic up to his throat and wrapping his arms tightly around his thin body, he squinted towards the east where the Golden Land lay thousands of miles beyond the vast, blue Pacific Ocean. The land where his great-grandfather had searched for gold. Where his grandfather had helped build a railroad. Where his father owned a restaurant. Now Kai was twelve years old, and it was his turn to journey to Gold Mountain. What would he find there?

Kai turned his thoughts to the morning he left home three weeks before. He remembered his mother's silence and her trembling hand as she served him his last breakfast of tea and rice porridge, cooked just the way he liked it – thick and steamy. He thought of his sister, Joy Yee, a small girl of eight years. Who would help her with her calligraphy now that he was gone? And when Kai thought of his grandmother, he squeezed his eyes tightly to hold back the tears. He could see her deep wrinkles like rivulets carved into her face. Mother and Joy Yee would come to *Gum San* one day, but Grandmother would never leave the land of her birth. When Kai said goodbye to her three weeks ago, she had taken his face in her withered hands and caressed his cheeks gently with her thumbs.

"Be a good boy," she whispered, "and do what your father tells you." Tears trickled down the soft lines of her face. Now, Kai swallowed hard just thinking about leaving her.

As Kai steamed away from his homeland, the wind whistling in his ears, his sadness mingled with new feelings of excitement. Would Father recognize him? Kai faintly remembered the gentle tone of Father's voice, but four years had erased most of his memories.

Kai thought back to Father's last visit to China four years earlier. He strode through the door wearing his funny, black hat, and his jolly laugh and warm embrace lit up their dim home. During this visit Father pulled Kai onto his lap, looked into his eyes, and told Kai that he would join him in America in four years, when he turned twelve. Back then the thought of America was nothing more than the sketches his father drew in the margins of his letters. Kai couldn't believe he would ever actually live there.

But that evening Kai overheard Grandmother arguing with Father about allowing Kai to journey to Gold Mountain. "Curse America!" she cried, clenching her fists. "The white devils will claim him forever, just as they have taken you and your father and your grandfather before you."

Kai's father shook his head and held his grandmother's steely gaze with his own ebony eyes. "Kai deserves to live with me in *Gum San* where he can get a proper education. He is the brightest boy here in Toy San. What future does he have in this poor village besides working in the rice paddies? Give him your blessing, Mother. I will not change my mind."

Grandmother stood silently as Father left the courtyard. He didn't look back. Kai crept to his sleeping mat mulling over their words. *Gum San*? White devils? Would he really live there some day?

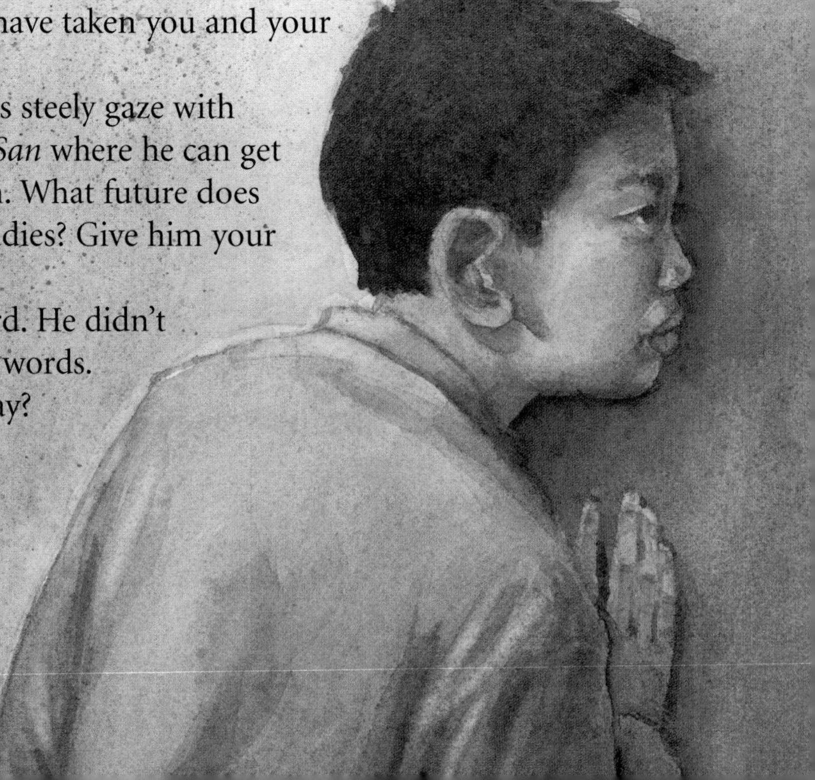

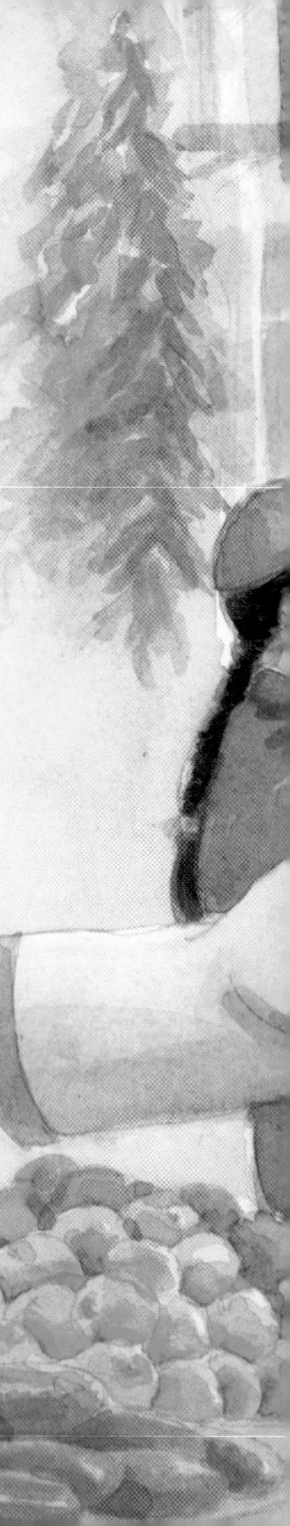

Now that Kai was finally on the ship, he could hardly believe it was only three weeks ago when he had waved goodbye to his home as his train left Toy San. The train took him to the fishing village of Buck Gai on the coast. There he boarded an overnight ferry to Hong Kong, where he spent nearly eighteen days waiting for his steamship, the *S.S. Hoover.* In Hong Kong he stayed with the *Gam San Jong*, an agent that helped Chinese travelers prepare their paperwork for the journey to America. The cold hands of a doctor probed Kai. Sharp needles stabbed him to ward off diseases on the ship. He purchased his crisp ticket with money Father had sent and studied the strange print on the ticket: *Hong Kong to San Francisco – July 8, 1934.*

While Kai waited for the boat to arrive, he explored the lively city of Hong Kong. He had never seen so many people bustling down crowded streets. Shops sold watches, fancy pens, cameras, and gadgets he hadn't known existed. Stalls overflowed with purple eggplants, dangling glazed chickens, and dried herbs. And tall buildings blocked out the rays of the sun. Best of all, he saw his first motion picture. *Mickey Mouse*! And one day he went to a tailor who made him a special American-style suit. The white shirt felt strange and stiff tucked into the wool pants. He loved the sound the zipper made as he pulled it up. He was used to a drawstring on his pants. Kai beamed as he looked in the tailor's mirror. He hardly recognized himself!

The giant body of the *S.S. Hoover* powered through the water breathing trails of black smoke like a dragon from its two tall stacks. Kai shared a third class cabin with five other young men. The cabin was dank and crowded with their six bunks and six suitcases. No fresh air or light flowed through its steel, gray walls. When Kai went to bed that first night, a scratchy, wool blanket kept him warm enough and a thin pillow cushioned his head. He ached from head to toe with homesickness as he fell asleep, cradled by the gentle rolling of the huge vessel.

On Board the *S.S. Hoover*

The next morning Kai explored the ship. He could see nothing but glassy, blue ocean stretching forever on all sides. Up on the deck he came upon a skinny boy who looked his age. The boy was watching a group of men playing cards. Eager for company, Kai pulled up a crate next to him. "Ni how ma! My name's Wong Kai Chong," he introduced himself. "What's yours?"

"I'm Young Jin Fong," the boy answered, nodding shyly.

Side by side, they watched the card game. After peppering him with questions, Kai learned that his quiet, new friend was born in the Year of the Dog, enjoyed playing games, and was going to live with his father in America. "Just like me!" Kai exclaimed.

That night the wind howled. Kai felt less alone since he had met Young. As he lay in his bunk, the *S.S. Hoover* tossed him from side to side. He fumbled under his pillow in the dark to find Father's letter. His thoughts drifted to a day two months ago, just after his twelfth birthday. That day he had come home after school and found a letter lying on the table. He picked it up and turned it over in his hands. A familiar stamp striped red, white, and blue sat in the corner, and Kai's name was written in Father's neat calligraphy across the front. How strange – usually letters from Father were addressed to Mother. Kai hesitated before opening it. He trembled, suspecting that once he opened the letter, his life would change forever.

Since Kai had left home, his father's letter had been his only comfort. In it was a long explanation preparing him for his trip to America. "The white devils have a law that makes it difficult for our people to enter Gold Mountain. You can only come because you are my son. Be ready to prove this to them." But how? Kai considered how little he knew of his father. He vaguely remembered his jolly laugh. He knew the sketches his father drew of his restaurant and the hilly streets of San Francisco. He knew the light in Mother's eyes when she read Father's letters to the family at dinner. These letters also meant meat on the table, a rare treat in Toy San. But he knew little else about Father. Kai was journeying to live with a man who was practically a stranger. Yet the officials in *Gum San* would expect him to prove that he was his son?

That night the knot in Kai's belly writhed like a snake.

The days on board the *S.S. Hoover* passed quickly. Kai loved the salty smell of the ocean and was relieved he wasn't seasick like many other passengers. His pale, moaning cabin mates hardly left their bunks. But Kai and Young met every morning after breakfast to watch the men play poker and checkers and *mah jong*. They spoke often of food, for the meals on the ship were poor.

"The first thing I'm going to eat at Father's restaurant is a large bowl of porridge, thick and steamy like Mother's!" Kai told Young.

"Not me," said Young. "I'm going to have beef with noodles."

"And roast duck. Covered in sweet plum sauce. When did I last have meat?" Kai wondered aloud.

They sighed and rubbed their stomachs longingly.

Several days later Kai came upon Young sitting in a corner of the deck studying a booklet of papers. Kai joined him and asked what he was reading. Young briskly closed the booklet, tucked it under his tunic, and walked away. Kai was surprised at Young's behavior. He must be hiding something. Kai decided not to ask any more questions. Grandmother had always told him to respect people's privacy.

Kai wondered if Young might be a paper son, like his neighbor's cousin, Wei. Wei's family had saved their money for six years to purchase papers claiming that his uncle, who lived in San Francisco, was his father. Wei studied his coaching papers carefully and practiced his new name. When he reached America he had to answer questions proving that he was his uncle's son. Kai was worried enough about his own interrogation to get into Gold Mountain, even though he truly was coming to live with his father. Imagine Young's fear if he was a paper son!

Altogether, the ship made three stops on its way to San Francisco. It stopped in Shanghai, in Tokyo, and in Honolulu. During each of these one-day stops, Kai and the other Chinese passengers looked longingly at the bustling port cities. They were not allowed to leave the *S.S. Hoover.*

Land!

A misty bank of fog greeted Kai on the morning of the twenty-first day of the journey. Cool droplets of damp air tickled his skin. When Kai squinted towards the horizon, as he had done every morning, his heart leapt. Out of the fog a dark mass was emerging. Land! White birds swooped playfully in the currents of wind next to the ship. Kai marveled at the steep, rocky cliffs looming in the mist as the *S.S. Hoover* entered San Francisco Bay. "Is this Gold Mountain?" he wondered. The seas were rough and the wind brisk. Shiny, gray heads peeked up from the waves. His father had sent sketches of these friendly creatures called seals. Kai laughed as a seal barked cheerfully, then disappeared under the white caps.

Kai looked up and saw Young standing at the railing. Young glanced nervously from left to right but didn't see Kai. When he thought no one was looking, Young quickly tossed his booklet of papers into the sea. Kai watched it disappear among the roiling foam. He sensed his friend's anxiety but knew it was best to allow Young to keep his secret. If he is a paper son, Kai thought, he will not want anyone to know. The risk of being caught and sent back to China is too great.

Kai pulled from his pocket Father's worn letter and read it once again: "Son, when your ship lands in San Francisco, the returning citizens and first class passengers will be allowed to land. But you will be taken to a place called Angel Island to be questioned by the *luk yi*. These men in green uniforms will interrogate you to prove whether or not you belong here. Don't be afraid. Know that you do belong here, for you are my son. Answer their questions honestly. If you do not know an answer, do the best you can. Be a good boy. Don't cause trouble. And I will be there at the pier to greet you when you are landed." Kai put the letter back in his pocket and closed his trembling fingers around it.

A tugboat guided the *S.S. Hoover* into the San Francisco pier. The passengers, crowded onto the upper decks, looked in silent wonder at the vast city before them. Kai thought of his father. Which of these hilly streets held his father's restaurant and Kai's new home?

As Kai stepped off the ship, green-clad guards directed the returning passengers to the right. They were quickly inspected and allowed to pass through. Kai was jostled to the left to wait on the docks with other Chinese travelers who didn't have any papers. The smell of fish from the many fishing boats nearby made Kai hold his breath. He saw Young and tried to wave, but Young didn't see him. He was looking nervously at the guards. So these were the white devils his grandmother had warned him about. Kai stared at them curiously. Up close, their faces were different from Chinese faces, especially their large noses!

Moments later, the *luk yi* herded Kai and the others onto a smaller boat. Soon he was headed back into the white-capped waves of the bay. Kai found Young on the deck of the ferry and stood by him. "The white devils must have strong senses of smell with noses like that," Kai joked. But Young could only force a smile.

The ferry docked at a big wooden landing in a sheltered cove of an island. As soon as the boat landed, more *luk yi* boarded and ordered Kai and his fellow passengers to disembark. "Why are they treating us like prisoners?" Young whispered anxiously to Kai. Kai shrugged his shoulders and cautioned Young with a "shh."

Island

Guards on the docks directed passengers lugging large suitcases and boxes to a white shed where they were ordered to pile their luggage. The weary travelers quickly opened their suitcases and removed a few necessities to bring with them. Since Kai's suitcase was so small, he was allowed to keep it.

While he waited, Kai looked up the long, broad pier at the buildings on the island. They were large and made of wood painted white and yellow. Four palm trees swayed in the wind, like serpents guarding a gate.

The guards beckoned the new arrivals to hurry and marched them up the long pier. Kai's knees wobbled as he shuffled along the firm boards. He looked over his shoulder at Young who was a few people behind him in the crowd. "Don't worry," he mouthed to his friend.

Kai followed the other new arrivals up a steep pathway to a large building on the hillside. They waited in line to sign their names in a black book. Then a man in a white coat gave an order that Kai did not understand. An interpreter translated the order: "Please remove your clothing for a medical examination." Kai gulped. He had never taken his clothes off in front of strangers before – especially white-faced strangers in white coats. Grandmother had always told him that the devil wore a white coat. White was the color of death. Kai remembered his father's warnings to be a good boy. Uneasily, he did as he was told. He kept his eyes cast downward and hugged his arms around his bare chest. When it was his turn, a white-coated man pressed a cold metal object onto his chest and gestured at Kai to breathe in and out. Then he lifted Kai's eyelids and peered into each of his eyes. Kai shuddered at how close he was to this foreign man. He could feel his breath on his face.

The next thing he knew, Kai was led into a cold, tiled room. More men in white coats stood by the doorway looking the new arrivals up and down and making notes on their clipboards. A pale, thin man near Kai buckled over in a fit of coughing that echoed through the room. One of the doctors pulled him aside and led him out the door. Kai stood up straight, inflated his chest, and did his best to appear healthy and strong. He did not want to be singled out for anything.

Suddenly showers of steaming water poured down from spouts in the ceiling. Kai gasped in surprise, but after a moment it felt good to be rinsed clean of the salt and grime from twenty-one days at sea. "This must be how the white devils bathe," he thought.

Doctors continued to inspect the new arrivals from head to toe as they dressed. Kai shivered. He put his clothes back on and escaped the hospital, relieved to have avoided any special attention.

The guards marched Kai and the other new arrivals up a long covered stairway into another large building on the opposite slope. Kai noticed thick, black wire criss-crossed on the windows. "Like cages," he thought. "But why? I have done nothing wrong." At the top of the stairs, Kai and the other men and boys were pointed to the left and the few women in their group were pointed to the right into a different part of the building. Seeing the women made him think of Mother, Grandmother, and Joy Yee. "If only they could be with me now," he wished.

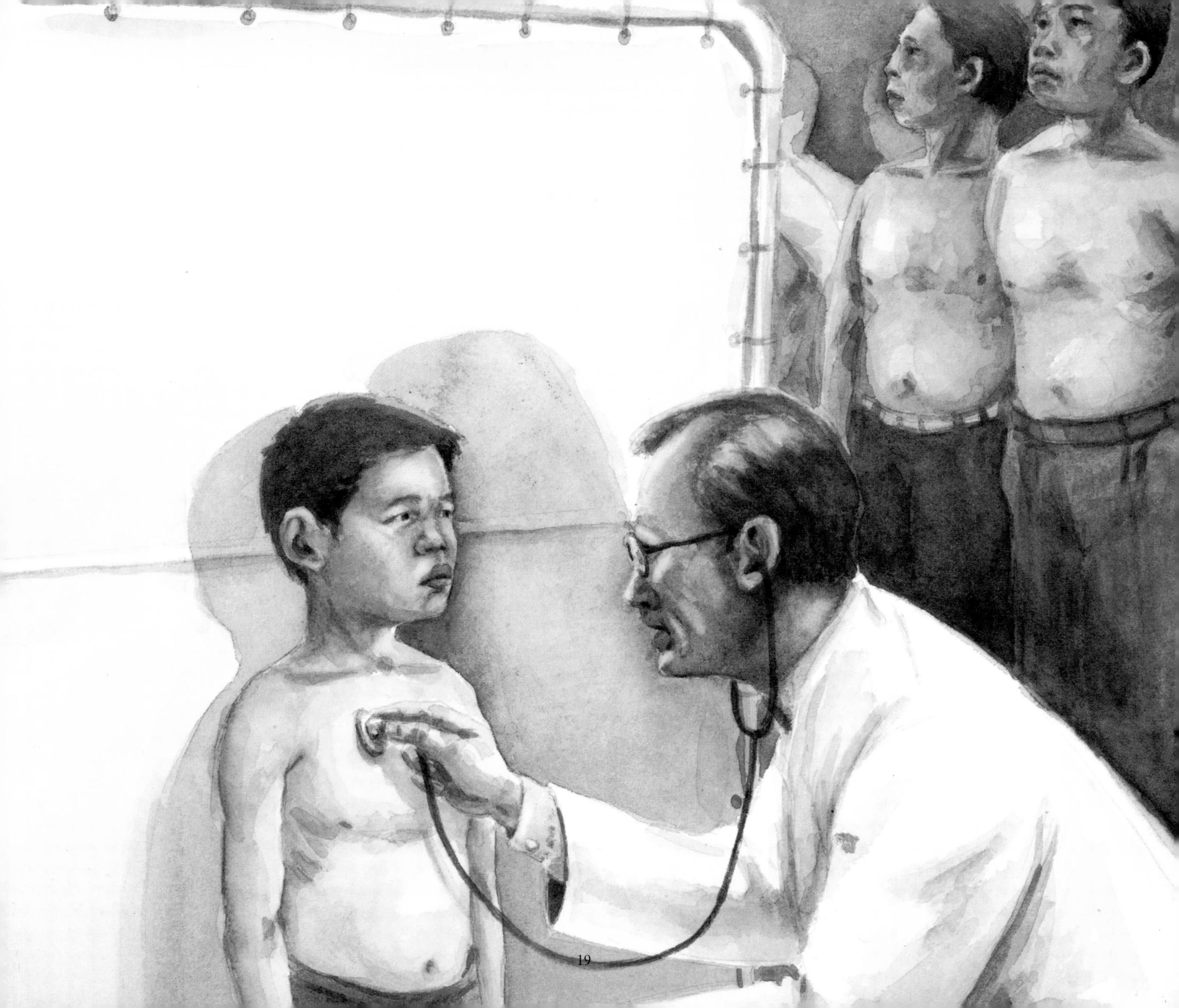

Kai's heart sank as he entered the huge room before him. He saw row upon row of metal bunk beds three tiers tall. Young men were lounging on their bunks, staring quietly at the newcomers. The air was stifling. Kai found a vacant bunk at the far left end of the room. He heard the door close. The clinking of the lock sent a shiver down his spine. Turning to face his bunk, he nodded a greeting to the older man sitting on the bottom bed. He climbed the metal ladder to the top bunk and lay down, exhausted from the day's events. "At least I will not be here for long," Kai assured himself. A mournful bell tolled in the distance as he fell asleep to the sounds of creaking beds, snoring, and sniffling.

Kai awoke with a start to a bellowing gong. Bunks squeaked and men sighed as they climbed down and pulled on their baggy trousers. Kai shivered in the morning's chill and damp. He tried not to disturb the old man below him as he stepped over him and made his way into the crowd flocking towards, what he hoped, was the place to eat. He saw Young in line and nudged his way forward so that they were standing shoulder to shoulder. Dark circles hung beneath Young's eyes.

The mess hall was a large room lined with long tables. As they took their seats, servers slammed down big bowls of rice porridge on each table. Starving, Kai dug in quickly. But it was watery and lukewarm – no better than the food on the ship. Kai forced it down, bite by bite, only by focusing on the memory of Mother's thick, steamy rice porridge. Utensils clanged against bowls, and the older men chattered, but Kai and Young ate quietly. They averted their eyes from the *luk yi* patrolling the aisles.

When Kai returned to the barracks after breakfast he noticed sunlight pouring through the door in the wall next to his bunk. He dashed over to it, hoping to take a walk and explore his new surroundings, free from the watchful eyes of the men in green. Instead he found only a small yard enclosed by a high, metal fence topped with sharp, pointy wire. A few older boys pushed past him and ran into the yard tossing a ball to each other. Kai called Young, and together they watched the game all morning. "They're trying to throw the ball into that basket on a pole," Young observed.

"Yes, and the other boys are blocking them. I am not tall like that basket, but I have good aim. And you are quick. We must learn this new game, Young," vowed Kai.

One day melted slowly into another on the island. Every night when Kai went to sleep he assured himself that he wouldn't be here much longer. He couldn't be. Every morning he awoke to the echoing gong. He ate breakfast. He learned to play basketball. More soggy rice with overcooked vegetables for lunch. Card games or *mah jong* all afternoon. Soggy rice with leftover vegetables for dinner. Lights out by 9:00. Scratchy phonographs of Chinese opera as he fell asleep. Day after day after day. This was not the life Kai had expected to find in Gold Mountain.

Kai wondered when his turn would come to be questioned by the immigration officers. After all, wasn't that why he was here? His father must be worried about him, but Kai had no way to contact him.

On some days the *luk yi* entered the barracks and called a name followed by the words, "*ho sai gai*." Whoops and cheers told Kai that someone had been released to land in San Francisco. On other days Kai watched the *luk yi* lead out men whose eyes flashed with the fury of caged tigers. Kai suspected that these men were being sent back to China. The mood of the barracks rose and fell with each day's news. The Chinese men in this room, though strangers, all shared the dream of reaching *Gum San*. For Kai, the worst part was the endless waiting. The man in the bunk below him had been on the island for twelve weeks, Kai learned. His graying head hung lower every day, and he rarely left his bunk.

夜靜微聞風嘯聲，
形影傷情見景詠。
雲霧潺潺也暗天，
蟲聲唧唧月微明。
悲苦相連天相遣，

One night Kai tossed and turned to the sounds of wind whistling through the bars outside his moonlit window. He awoke with a start to a noise like a rat scratching its claws against the wall. He peered nervously down to the bunk below, holding his breath. What was this? Kai's bunkmate was etching something into the wall behind their bed. How strange! He was working so intently that he didn't notice Kai. What could the old man be writing? Relieved that it wasn't a rat, but puzzled, Kai lay awake listening through the night.

In the morning Kai waited until the old man had left for breakfast. As soon as the barracks were empty he looked on the wall behind his bunk and found it covered in Chinese script. His eyes followed the rows of the old man's poem down the wall:

In the quiet of the night, I heard, faintly, the
whistling of wind.
The forms and shadows saddened me;
The floating clouds, the fog, darken the sky.
The moon shines faintly as the insects chirp.
The sad person sits alone, leaning by a window.

Kai sat very still contemplating Angel Island. Father had said nothing in his letter about this locked room with sad poetry on its walls. Kai dragged his feet down the covered walkway to breakfast, aching for home and feeling terribly alone.

One sunny morning several weeks later, Kai was playing basketball with Young and the other boys in the yard. As he shot the ball towards the basket, something caught his eye beyond the tall fence: a tree with purple fruits dangling from its branches. Plums! He ran over to the fence and jumped to reach one of the fruits, but he missed. Kai thought of his boring diet of soggy rice and overcooked vegetables. He dreamed of the plum sauce he would have with duck at Father's restaurant. The plums swayed in the breeze just beyond his grasp. Sweet and tempting. "Hmm," Kai thought. "There must be a way…"

He ran inside to his bunk and grabbed a pair of old trousers. Hurrying back to the yard, he tied knots at the cuffs of the pants to make them into a sack. He called Young and whispered his plan into his friend's ear. Young grinned. Then they took the pants and pushed them under the fence near the fruit tree. They rejoined the game of basketball, and as soon as Kai got the ball, he winked at Young and threw the ball up and over the fence towards the plum tree. "Hey, *luk yi!*" he cried to the guard lounging by the gate. Kai motioned towards the ball with his arms, shrugged his shoulders, and with a questioning glance, asked the guard to help.

The lazy guard barked something that Kai didn't understand, but he unlocked the gate and pointed to Kai and Young to get the ball. With innocent looks on their faces, they sped around behind the fence where they found their sack on a carpet of ripe, fallen plums. Scrambling, they filled their bag with fruit in moments. They squeezed it under the fence, found the basketball under the tree, and returned to the gate before the guard became suspicious. Once inside, the boys scurried to the fence, retrieved the bag of fruits, and snuck it into the barracks to feast upon the sweet, purple plums. Sticky juice ran down their chins, as they laughed and laughed.

Five weeks passed. Every day Kai clung to the hope of being released. "Just one more day," he assured himself. "Don't give up on me, Father," he wished as he fell asleep each night, fingering the tattered letter under his pillow.

The Interrogation

One foggy morning in August when Kai was playing basketball, he heard his name called in an unfamiliar voice. Dropping the ball, he raced inside to find a guard waiting by the door. The time for his interrogation had finally come! He fumbled on his buttons as he quickly changed into his gray suit from Hong Kong. He smoothed his black hair with his hand. Taking a deep breath, he reminded himself not to worry. He was a legitimate son of a citizen and had nothing to fear. Young's glance revealed a tinge of envy as Kai passed his bunk, half-running to meet the *luk yi*, whose black boot tapped impatiently by the door.

Kai's interrogation began smoothly. A tall, stern white devil wearing a wool suit asked all the questions in English. A Chinese man, also dressed in a suit, translated everything the tall man said to Kai. A uniformed guard hovered nearby. A female white devil, the first Kai had seen, sat clicking her fingertips on a black machine while Kai and the men spoke.

They began with basic questions. What were all his names? How old was he? What was the name of his village? What were the names of all his family members? How old were they? For how long had his father been in America? Where did he live? What was his job? After answering their many questions with ease, Kai began to relax. Surely he would pass.

But suddenly the questions became more difficult. “How many chairs were in your house in China?”

“What a strange question,” Kai puzzled. It was a small house. Four people lived in it. Plus his father when he visited. So there were probably five chairs. “Five,” Kai guessed.

“What did the chairs look like? Were their backs round or square?”

“Square,” replied Kai. He clasped and unclasped his sticky palms in his lap.

The interrogator shot Kai an accusing look. “Interesting,” he replied, tapping his pen on the desk. “That’s not what your father said.” Kai’s heart leapt. These men had spoken with his father! The thought of Father strengthened him. Taking a deep breath, he replied again.

“Sir, to the best of my knowledge, the chairs were square.” Kai remembered how Father had warned him not to cause trouble. But he knew that one mistake could fail his interrogation. Could send him back to China. Oh, the shame this would cause Father. Kai thought of his grandmother’s words. “Be a good boy.” He searched the interrogator’s face for a sign of understanding. “I apologize for arguing, sir, but I lived in that house and sat on those chairs every day. My father lives here in America and only returns to China every four years. Who do you think knows the chairs better - him or me?” He swallowed. “Believe me. They’re square.”

With that, the interrogator raised his eyebrows to the guard and the translator. They looked at the small, bold boy sitting erect in his chair. And gradually a smile broke out on the interrogator’s face. The translator glanced sideways at him and chuckled. Even the guard joined in their laughter and winked at Kai. Kai didn’t dare smile in the presence of the white devils, but relief washed over him.

"Ho Sai Gai!"

After his interrogation Kai waited and waited. He tossed restlessly at night. He perched on the edge of his bunk during the day. He didn't even play basketball for fear of missing his news. Then, on the morning of the fourth day of waiting, a guard entered the barracks after breakfast and looked down towards Kai's bunk in the corner. "Wong Kai Chong?" Kai looked up. A ray of sunlight streamed in from the open door. The room fell silent. "*Ho sai gai!*" Kai paused in disbelief. Me? I have been landed?

He scrambled down from the top bunk. The old man below stood to face Kai and gently squeezed his shoulders. The boys from the bunks nearby swarmed around him patting him on the back and congratulating him. Kai was overjoyed. His knees shook. But a nagging feeling held him back. Kai could see an envious longing in the boys' faces, despite their generous smiles. He was free to go home to his father, but they were staying behind. Some might even be sent back to China. Kai bowed to each of them solemnly.

Once he had his gray suit on, his few belongings packed, and his suitcase in hand, he turned to face the guard waiting for him by the open door. But wait! Where was Young? He looked towards Young's bunk and saw his friend sitting cross-legged staring out the barred window. The guard cleared his throat impatiently. Kai called Young's name, but Young wouldn't look up. Kai understood. He whispered, "Goodbye. Good luck to you, my friend," even though Young probably wouldn't hear him. He hoped that Young would hear the call, "*Ho sai gai*," soon. Maybe they would meet again. He turned to the open door, and the guard ushered him out of the barracks into the sunshine.

Kai jogged to keep up with the guard's strides. Down on the docks he saw the same small boat that had brought him to this island six long weeks ago. He was on his way to San Francisco to find his father, at last.

Kai looked back at Angel Island disappearing behind a bank of fog. In his mind he could hear the nighttime sounds of scratchy Chinese opera, creaking metal bunks, and sniffling. He remembered the old man etching his sad poem onto the wall. He cringed remembering all the soggy rice. The embarrassing medical exam. The boredom. He smiled thinking of basketball, especially the day he and Young discovered the plums. Shuddering at the thought of his friend having to stay behind on Angel Island, he hoped that Young would pass the interrogation soon.

Kai's heart pounded as the ferry approached the docks in San Francisco. He pushed his hair out of his eyes. He tugged at his new suit's sleeves, which were already getting too short. He inhaled the salty air deeply and pushed back his shoulders, wanting to show his father how much he had grown. Squinting into the sunlight, he searched for Father among the small crowd of people on the pier. Would he be there? Kai craned his neck to find him.

Just then he saw a figure running along the wharf waving a black, felt hat. He heard a jolly laugh. "Kai! Wong Kai Chong!"

"Father!" Kai cried. He pulled the letter from his pocket and waved it in the air.

The boat seemed to take forever to land. Finally, the railing was lifted. Kai leapt off the ferry's ramp, pushed through the crowd, and stood face to face with his father. He bowed respectfully, but Father stepped towards him and took him into his arms. Protective, familiar arms. And as they stood there amidst the bustle of the docks, Kai knew, at last, that he had found Gold Mountain.

Kai (now called Albert) tells his story (right)

Immigrants arrive at Angel Island (left)

Kai's immigration and passport photos (below)

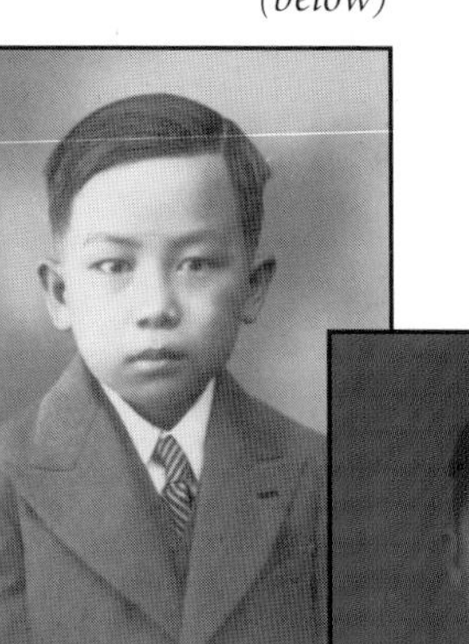

Kai with his family:
His brother (right), his father (left), and his mother (bottom right)

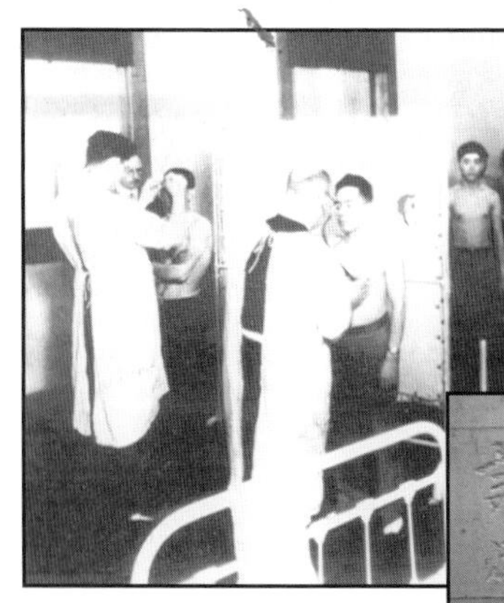

Medical exams for immigrants

本屋拘留幾十天
所因墨例致牽連
可惜英雄無用武
只聽音來策祖鞭
從今遠別此樓中
各位鄉君衆歡同
莫道其間皆西式
設成玉砌變如籠

A poem carved on the wall of the Immigration Station at Angel Island

Historical Notes

Kai's Journey to Gold Mountain is based primarily on the experiences of my friend, Albert "Kai" Wong. The story also includes elements from oral histories of other Chinese immigrants.

Albert in 2004

- Albert "Kai" Wong, came to America on the *S.S. Hoover* in 1934 for a better education and to live with his father. His father accompanied him on the voyage from China to San Francisco. However, many children Kai's age did make the journey alone.

- Kai met a friend named Young on the ship. Young may or may not have been a paper son. Many Chinese did come to America as paper sons or daughters. They purchased "coaching papers" to study and often tossed them into the ocean before arriving so as not to be discovered.

Albert with his grandson

- Kai and Young learned to play basketball on Angel Island and did indeed discover a plum tree. Kai later became the captain of the San Jose High School basketball team, not because he was tall but because he had an accurate shot. One day at an All-Star game in 1939, he bumped into his old friend, Young. At the age of eighty, Kai still plays basketball nearly every day in San Francisco's Chinatown.

- Kai's mother, sisters, and brothers came to California in 1938. He never saw his grandmother again. She died shortly after he left China.

- The Chinese Exclusion Act, passed in 1882, was designed to keep the Chinese from entering the United States unless they were merchants, scholars, or sons or daughters of residents. This law was not repealed until 1943 when the U.S. was allied with China during World War II.

- Many detainees at Angel Island carved poems into the walls of the barracks to express their feelings while they waited to be landed. You can see these poems if you visit the island today.

About the Author

Katrina Currier grew up in Massachusetts and was first introduced to Angel Island when it became part of the social studies curriculum in the Newton Public Schools, where she taught fourth grade. Surprised at the shortage of children's literature about Angel Island, she began this book when she moved to San Francisco in 2001. Through her research, she met Albert "Kai" Wong, who generously shared his story with her.

Katrina lives in San Francisco with her husband and two young sons. This is her first picture book for children.

About the Illustrator

Gabhor Utomo lived in Indonesia until 1997, when he moved to San Francisco to study at the Academy of Art College. He received his Bachelor of Fine Arts in Illustration in 2003. Gabhor's 13-year-old friend, Anton, served as his model for Kai.

Gabhor lives with his wife, Dina, in San Francisco. This is his first picture book for children.

For further information:

Angel Island Association
P.O. Box 866
Tiburon CA 94920
www.angelisland.org

Angel Island Immigration Station Foundation
P.O. Box 29237
San Francisco CA 94129-0237
www.aiisf.org